HINKL

And Other
Shlemiel Stories

Also by Miriam Chaikin:

Make Noise, Make Merry
Ask Another Question
Sound The Shofar
Shake A Palm Branch
Light Another Candle
Joshua In The Promised Land
Aviva's Piano
I Should Worry, I Should Care
Finders, Weepers
Getting Even
Lower! Higher! You're A Liar!
How Yossi Beat The Evil Urge
Yossie Asks The Angels For Help
The Seventh Day

HINKL

And Other *Shlemiel* Stories

Miriam Chaikin

Drawings by Marcia Posner

6

A Shapolsky Book
Published by Shapolsky Publishers

For any additional information, contact:
Shapolsky Publishers, Inc.
56 East 11th Street, New York, NY 10003

Designed by Malcolm Jordan-Robinson

10 9 8 7 6 5 4 3 2 1

First Edition 1987

Library of Congress Cataloging in Publication Data
Chaikin, Miriam
HINKL And Other Shlemiel Stories

ISBN 0-933503-15-6

"Hinkl" © 1983, reprinted from *Young Judea Magazine.*
"'Me Too! Me Too!' Said Gamani" © 1984, reprinted from *Young Judea Magazine.*
"Yussie, The Locksmith" © 1972, reprinted from *The Happy Pair and Other Love Stories,* G. P. Putnam's Sons.
"Feet In, Feet Out" © 1986, reprinted from *Young Judea Magazine.*
"Ittki, Pittki" © 1971, Parents' Magazine Press.
"Hardlucky" © 1973, J. B. Lippincott Co.

For Benny, Shami, Payoo and Yuss.

Contents

(About a *shlemiel* who got a telegram.)

(Talk about *shlemiels*? Here's a pair.)

Yussie, The Locksmith   39

(He found the key to stop being a *shlemiel.*)

Feet In, Feet Out   53

(About a whole town full of *shlemiels*.)

(A *shlemiel* who was afraid to offend a prince.)

(A *shlemiel* who "made it.")

Hinkl

You hear stories about the fools of Chelm. But fools don't live only in Chelm. They live everywhere. If you doubt it, just look around.

Take Hinkl.

For the life of him, Hinkl couldn't learn to sit down. For years people showed him how. "Walk up to the chair," they said. "Touch it with your knees, to make sure it's there. About Face. Sit." He never caught on. Never got the hang of it. Somehow, each time he went to sit, he landed on the floor. After a while he stopped trying.

Now, Hinkl never sits. He eats standing up, like a horse. If he wants to rest, he leans against the wall, like a shovel. Is that a way to rest? Of course not. A person has to sit to rest. That's why we have all that padding down there. But poor Hinkl. He can't rest. He is always tired.

His aunt, Raizl-the-dressmaker, with whom he
lives, worries herself sick over him. How will he
work? Who will ever marry him? Each time she
glances up from her sewing and sees him leaning
against the wall, she sighs and shakes her head.
"He is only fifteen," she says to herself. "But he
looks like an old man."

One day, Hinkl had a stroke of luck. Velvel's
chicken plucker died. And Velvel, the owner of the
poultry market, needed a new plucker. The job
wasn't for everyone. But it was perfect for Hinkl.

Velvel was a bit stingy. He owned one stool. One.
O-N-E. Only he was allowed to sit on it. When he
closed the market, he took it upstairs, to his house.
In the morning he brought it down again. As Hinkl
needed no chair and wouldn't start trouble about a
place to sit, Velvel hired him right away.

Velvel taught Hinkl how to pluck a chicken. He
watched Hinkl like a hawk. The first time Velvel
looked away, Hinkl threw out the plucked chicken
and put the feathers on the counter to sell. Velvel
caught it in time. (Don't worry, those stingies have
eyes in the backs of their heads.)

After a few days, Hinkl and Velvel were as happy
as could be. It was a match made in heaven. Hinkl
didn't have any chairs around to remind him that
he couldn't sit. And Velvel had no reason to feel
stingy.

Hinkl was glad to be a worker, and it showed. He

began to blossom. He earned three pipki a week. (It wasn't much. How far is three from zero? Still, it was something.) Two pipki he gave to his aunt, to pay for his room and board. And one pipki he kept for himself.

Now that Hinkl had a job, Raizl, his aunt, thought he should get married. So what if he didn't know how to sit? He was kind. He was generous. He was working. A girl could do worse.

Raizl sent for Zitka, the marriage broker. Zitka knew of three girls who were looking for husbands and went to see them.

"Hinkl?" said one. "But he's over fifty!"

"The chicken plucker? Feh!" said another.

"Pugh!" said the third, holding her nose and looking away.

Raizl didn't let on that she was disappointed. Neither did Hinkl. He would have liked to get married so he could go to a wedding. But he acted like he didn't care.

One day one of Raizl's customers brought in a dress to fix. The customer kept raisins in the pocket of her dress, so she would always have something to eat. She decided to go on a diet and asked Raizl to sew up the pockets, so she couldn't get at the raisins. (Talk about fools.)

Raizl discussed Hinkl with the customer and the customer told Raizl about a surgeon in the capital. Raizl didn't know what a surgeon was. The customer explained, saying a surgeon was a doctor who could cut and sew, like herself, and make long noses smaller.

The capital was fifty miles away. It meant a long voyage on a dusty train. But, being a dressmaker, Raizl undestood the power of a stitch. On Hinkl's day off she bought one seat for herself, and got on the train with Hinkl.

The surgeon listened to Raizl, then said: "Why does he have to sit? Let him lie down if he wants to rest."

Poor Raizl! Poor Hinkl! Fifty miles on a dusty train to hear that! (Don't worry, there are plenty of fools among doctors.) Raizl and Hinkl got back on the dusty train.

On the way to the capital the conductor didn't bother Hinkl. He let him stand. But the conductor on the way back told Hinkl he couldn't stand. Hinkl said he couldn't sit. The conductor took a pamphlet from his back pocket and read aloud:

"Every passenger must have a seat."

Hinkl repeated that he couldn't sit.

The conductor stomped away, ripped out an empty seat, and gave it to Hinkl.

"Every passenger must have a seat," he repeated, and went on his way without charging Hinkl for the seat. (*Nu, nu!* And what would you call him?)

Raizl and Hinkl reached home. Time passed. Nothing happened. Then one day when it looked like nothing was going to happen again, something happened.

It was lunch time in the market. Velvel was upstairs with his stool, eating. There were no customers in the market. Hinkl stood leaning against the door with a toothpick in his mouth, watching the street. Suddenly, an old peddler with a heavy pack on his back entered the market. He removed the pack from his back and sighed wearily.

"I have been walking all day," he said. "May I sit down to rest for a while?"

"There's no place to sit here," Hinkl said.

The old man glanced around. "Where do you sit?"

"I don't sit."

"What do you mean, you don't sit?"

"I never sit."

"But how can that be?" the old man asked. "A person our age has to sit down once in a while."

Hinkl didn't like being taken for an old man.

"I'm a young boy," he said.

The old man examined Hinkl's face closely. "I see you are telling the truth," he said. "How did this happen?"

Hinkl explained. In the next moment, the market was abuzz with noise and people. The boy from the telegraph office came in with a telegram for Hinkl and half the town followed him in to see what the telegram said.

Hinkl took the telegram and looked at it, turning it this way and that.

"Open it!" someone called.

"Read it!" called another.

Hinkl looked at the peddler. "Do you know how to read?" he asked.

The peddler took the envelope, opened it, and read aloud:

"WE ARE PLEASED TO ANNOUNCE THAT YOUR GREAT UNCLE HAS DIED AND LEFT YOU FIFTY PIPKI. THE LAWYERS."

People began to cheer and yell. Hinkl couldn't believe his good fortune. He looked around, stunned.

The peddler threw open his pack and spread his wares out on the floor. "You're rich, Hinkl," he said. "Buy yourself a present. A watch. Cufflinks. Something."

"Go ahead, Hinkl," the people called.

Hinkl bent to look over the wares. As he glanced over the things he saw his face reflected back in a shiny new pot. He was smiling! He had never seen himself smile before. He picked up the pot and looked into it. Not only was he able to see his face in it, he could see the crate with live chickens, behind him. His heart exploded with joy. He could see behind himself!

The peddler saw right away what was what. "Wait," he said, taking the pot from Hinkl. He snipped off some wire from a roll, twisted it into

loops and attached it to the pot. Everyone watched in silence, Hinkl too. Then, as if the loops were sleeves, he slipped Hinkl's arms through them. Hinkl stood smiling up into the pot.

"What is he doing. . . . ?" people asked.

"Some contraption. . . ." someone said.

"*Nu,* Hinkl?" the peddler said.

Hinkl nodded. "Watch this," he said with a grin and walked slowly backwards. He stopped at the crate. Slowly, slowly, he lowered himself.

Hinkl was sitting! Everyone began to cheer. The chickens in the crate squawked and nipped at him through the slits. But did Hinkl care? Not at all. He was sitting! For the first time in his life, he was sitting.

The noise from the market brought the rest of the town running. Velvel came down with his stool. Someone ran to get Raizl and she arrived out of breath and still holding the skirt she was hemming.

The peddler took advantage of the excitement to sit for a while on Velvel's stool.

From that day on, business at the market jumped. People came not only to buy chickens but to see Hinkl's contraption. Business was so good, Velvel bought a new stool for himself and gave Hinkl the old one.

Now that Hinkl could rest he began to look a little better. The three girls that Zitka had gone to see were still not interested in marrying him, but Zitka had found a new girl. The girl had seen Hinkl in the market and fallen in love with him. She was not young. And she was far from pretty. But she smiled without end and had good, strong teeth.

Arrangements were made for the wedding.

And what a wedding it was! Hinkl had no need for his contraption that night. He danced all night long, with the bride, with his mother-in-law, with his aunt, with Zitka, and sometimes, out of pure joy, by himself.

"Me Too! Me Too!"
Said Gamani

Once in Petak Tikvah there lived a rich man, Ashir by name. As rich as he was, that's how foolish he was. Whatever anyone owned, he had to have one too, only bigger.

His wife, Gamani, wasn't much better. She had a different *mishugass* (Yiddish for "craziness"). If anyone said this or that, she had one answer: "Me too! Me too!" A trait like that leads to trouble. Already, on account of her *me-tooing,* one room was full of turtles, another was full of water, and another had no floor.

One day Ashir and Gamani stood outside watching a parade in honor of an American who had come to visit. Ashir heard the man behind him say, "That gold button the American is wearing is the largest gold button ever."

Ashir pricked up his ears. "Really, the largest

ever?'' he asked.

"The largest ever,'' the man repeated.

Nothing else would do. Ashir had to have a gold button that was even larger. He ran to the button merchant and told him what he wanted.

"We work with cloth here, not gold,'' the merchant said. "Try the jeweler.''

Ashir hurried to the jeweler. The jeweler too said it was not a matter for him but one for the goldsmith.

"You have come to the right place,'' said the goldsmith, one eye on the cash drawer and drumming on his chest with his fingertips. "Your gold button will be ready in the morning.''

On steps light as air, Ashir went home.

Gamani spent the day walking arm-in-arm with her friend, Mrs. Tipshi. Before going home, they stopped at a cafe for ice cream.

"Two scoops of vanilla, with chocolate chips and nuts—not too many nuts,'' Mrs. Tipshi told the waiter.

"Me too,'' Gamani said.

"I don't like it too sweet,'' Mrs. Tipshi said to Gamani.

"Me too,'' Gamani answered.

When they finished eating, Mrs. Tipshi said the ice cream had left too sweet a taste in her mouth. She rolled her tongue over her teeth and said a nice, salty herring would get rid of the taste.

"I wish I had a barrelful of herring," she said to Gamani.

"Me too. Me too," said Gamani.

"Gamani!" Ashir called as he entered the house. "Tomorrow I will own the largest gold button ever!"

Gamani gave him a smile and went out onto the balcony. Ashir followed her. "What is this?" he asked, gazing at a large wooden barrel.

"Herring," she said.

"Herring?"

Gamani told her husband what had happened. She gazed at the barrel and turned up her nose.

"It smells so," she said.

"I will remove the smell," Ashir said.

He instructed a servant to chop down the balcony with an ax and the servant did so. He then arranged the table on the rubble and served Ashir and Gamani their supper.

In the morning, Ashir hurried to the goldsmith. He trembled with joy as an enormous gold button hanging on a pink velvet string was placed around his neck. It was heavy and Ashir could hardly stand under the weight. But what did it matter? He was now the owner of the largest gold button ever. Happy, Ashir paid for the button and left.

Outside, he ran into a friend.

"Ashir, that's a nice gold button you have there," the friend said.

"This is the largest gold button ever," Ashir said, trying to raise his head.

"It's a peanut compared to the Australian's," the friend said.

Sputtering and choking, Ashir faced about and marched himself back to the goldsmith's.

"Of course the Australian's gold button is larger," the goldsmith said. "You asked for a button that was larger than the American's." He jabbed Ashir in the button. "And that's what we gave you."

"I want a gold button larger than the Australian's!" Ashir said.

"Why didn't you say so in the first place?" the goldsmith said. "We'll have it for you in the morning."

Ashir walked home with a straight back, content. He was greeted at the door by a baby goat.

"Isn't he cute?" Gamani asked, stepping out from behind the drapes.

"Where did he come from?" Ashir asked.

Gamani told him.

"I was at the bazaar with Mrs. Tipshi. The cutest little baby goat was running loose. It came up to us. 'How adorable,' Mrs. Tipshi said. 'I wish I had one at home.' And I . . ."

"I know," Ashir finished. "You said, 'Me too. Me too.'"

Gamani smiled and looked affectionately at the little goat.

"And where will it sleep?" Ashir asked. "We have run out of rooms because of your *me-tooing*."

Gamani's face fell.

"Never mind," Ashir said, tucking her under the chin. "We'll find a place for him."

They sat down to a fine meal that the servant had prepared and Ashir proceeded to tell Gamani about his day.

The next morning, Ashir could again be seen hurrying through the streets. He gasped at the sight that greeted him at the goldsmith's shop. Propped up against the wall was what surely had to be the largest gold button ever. The goldsmith and his assistant huffed and puffed as they lifted the gold button over Ashir's head. Ashir was bent over double. But of what importance was that? He owned the largest gold button ever.

Slowly, shuffling along, Ashir made his way home. As he opened the door, honey cakes came flying at him. The floor was strewn with them. He could not look up. But he had a good view of the floor. He saw Gamani's feet rush by. Then the servant's. He watched from between his legs as both ran frantically with buckets, trying to catch the flying cakes.

"What's going on?" he asked.

"The servant was baking," Gamani said. "And he said he wished the oven could do its own baking, without his help."

"And she said, 'Me too! Me too!'" the servant added. "And all at once the oven began to spit out cakes."

Ashir always had a ready solution for most things. But he could not think of anything to do against the flying cakes. "Let's move," he said.

That's what they did. That very night.

Ashir lay in his new bedroom, gazing at the gold button propped up against the wall. The sight made him happy. Thinking fondly of himself, he fell asleep.

In the morning, wearing his gold button, he went out into the street expecting to be admired. His only regret was that no one could see the proud expression on his face. Suddenly he no longer felt proud. His chin scraped the ground. Behind him was an Arab wearing a gold button that was larger than his own.

Fuming and sputtering, Ashir returned to the goldsmith's shop.

"That would have been the sheik," said the goldsmith. "Everyone knows he owns the largest gold button ever. You asked for one that was larger than the Australian's. And that's what we gave you."

Ashir could not argue. He had received exactly what he had asked for each time. "Help me," he pleaded. "I will not rest until I own the largest gold button ever."

The goldsmith cocked an eye at the cash drawer and drummed his fingers on his chest.

"Please..." Ashir said. "I'll do anything..."

The goldsmith bent to look Ashir in the eye. "Anything?" he asked.

Ashir nodded, trying not to let his chin scrape the ground.

The goldsmith and his assistant removed Ashir's button.

"Very well," said the goldsmith. "You know the empty lot next to the blacksmith's?"

Ashir nodded.

"Meet us there at dawn, but speak of it to no one," the goldsmith said.

A river of excitement ran through Ashir as he wended his way home. He was so pleased with his good fortune that it was evening before he realized that he hadn't seen Gamani. He asked the servants, but no one knew where she was.

Eager to greet the morning, Ashir got ready for bed. As he went to close the shutters, Gamani came floating by outside.

What happened to you?" Ashir asked.

Gamani explained. "Mrs. Tipshi said today that she envied the clouds their freedom. She wished she were as free as a cloud...." Gamani did not finish the sentence. She became wispy and drifted away. Ashir was just as glad. He had promised not to speak of his plan to anyone.

The morning found Ashir hurrying through the dark streets, to the empty lot.

Ashir gasped when he saw what was waiting for him. Surely there could be no bigger gold button in all the world.

The goldsmith's assistant climbed up the button and the goldsmith handed Ashir up to him. The assistant fastened Ashir to the button with ropes and pulleys, then climbed back down again.

"Congratulations!" the men called up to Ashir as they left.

Ashir thanked them and waved goodbye. Tears of happiness filled his eyes.

"At last, I have what I want," he said.

"Me too! Me too!" said the little cloud that floated by.

Yussie,
the Locksmith

Once, in the downtown section of a large city, there lived a man named Yussie, a locksmith by trade. He fixed locks and made keys. You could see him, early in the morning, sitting in the window of his store and picking at a broken lock. You could see him there late at night, too.

Because he was a good locksmith, Yussie had plenty of work. But that isn't what kept him in the store. The fact is he hated to go upstairs. That's where he lived with Rosie, his wife. Red Rosie is what the neighbors called her, on account of the color of her hair. Her temper had a lot to do with it, too. It didn't take much to make Red Rosie mad.

On the plus side, she was a good cook. One look at her angel food cake was enough to make your mouth water. And the house was spotless. "You could eat off her floors," the neighbors said. More than once, when she refused to let him sit at the table, Yussie had to do just that.

On the minus side was her temper and the fact that she was always arguing. For one thing, she would have liked to move to a better neighborhood, where there was a tree. But Yussie couldn't afford it.

"You don't get rich being a locksmith," he would say.

"So be something else," she would answer.

"But a locksmith is what I am," he would say.

"*A nobody* is what you are," she would answer.

And so it went.

One fine morning Yussie got up earlier than usual. He tiptoed around, trying not to wake his wife. Things were peaceful when she was asleep. And he was in a good mood because spring had come. At the end of the day, when he finished his work, he would take a chair outside and sit in front of the store. He looked forward to that. There was nothing he liked better, when the weather was nice, than to sit and watch the people go by.

He heard a sudden clump in the bedroom and flinched. Rosie was up! He was hoping to be downstairs in the store before she got up. Well, what was she going to find to argue about this morning?

"You want to take a bath first?" he asked, avoiding one argument.

"You go first," she said. "I'll make breakfast."

Avoiding another argument, Yussie was in and out of the tub in no time. As he sat on the bed and finished dressing, he heard his wife in the bathroom, running water for her own bath. So he was surprised to see her suddenly standing in front of him with her arms crossed and her mouth pulled over to the side.

"You used up all the hot water," she said.

"I'm sorry," Yussie said and bent down to put on his shoes.

"I'm sorry," she mimicked and snatched the shoes out of his hands. And when he went into the kitchen and sat down at the table to eat his breakfast, she snatched the plate away from under his nose.

"Out!" she said, opening the door to the store and pointing downstairs.

What could he do? In his stocking feet, he went downstairs. He put the OPEN FOR BUSINESS sign in the window and began to sweep up. Soon Pat, the policeman, came in with a broken lock. Yussie tried to keep his feet out of sight so Pat shouldn't see that he was shoeless. But Pat never noticed. He showed Yussie how the lock was sticking, and left.

When Pat left, Yussie went behind the counter, where he worked, and sat down on his high stool near the window. He looked over the counter: twelve keys to make, seven locks to fix, and three nameplates to press out. He shook his head, wondering where to begin, and began to make a new key. He was glad to be busy. It kept his mind off his feet. Off his stomach, too. He was starving.

Someone knocked on the window and Yussie looked up. Zalman, the old clothes dealer, was standing outside and waving. With him was his nephew, the fat one. Yussie gave them a smile and waved back. He watched them move on, then returned to his work.

As he was picking at a lock, he could hear his wife upstairs. She was slamming drawers and banging stuck jars against the wall. *What is she so angry about?* he asked himself. *Her feet are in shoes! She had breakfast!*

When noon came, Yussie didn't know what to

do. He usually went upstairs for lunch. But today he didn't dare. He looked down at his feet. He couldn't go out, either. Suddenly the delicious smell of baking came wafting down the stairs. Yussie sniffed at the air. *Angel food cake!* His favorite!

"Can I come up, Rosie?" he called.

"Who is speaking?" her voice called back.

"I'm hungry," he said.

"Brains you need, not food," she answered.

"Have a heart, I'm starving," he said.

"Starving?" She gave a false laugh. "A *nobody* is made of air. How can a *nobody* starve?"

"...throw me down my shoes so I can go out and eat," he said, getting angry.

"A *nobody* doesn't need shoes, either," she said and slammed the door shut.

"Loxenkeys!" Yussie cried and gave the counter a slap. "Loxenkeys" is always what he said when he was angry. And the counter is always who he slapped. (Who else should he slap? Red Rosie? Who would dare!)

Stuck is stuck, he thought, looking down at his feet. He glanced out the window to see whom he could ask to bring him a sandwich. Bennie, the knife sharpener, whose horse and wagon were usually outside, was nowhere around. Neither was the boy next door who was always throwing a ball against the stoop.

The landlord went by, looked in, and waved.

Yussie waved back. While his hand was still in the air, he waved at the Assemblyman, who went by next. Yussie wondered what would happen if he asked the Assemblyman to bring him a sandwich. The thought made him smile. You don't ask people in high places to bring you a sandwich.

The upstairs door banged open again. "Hey, Mr. *Nobody*!" his wife's voice called. Yussie decided not to answer. *Let her call her head off,* he thought. Then he wondered if she had forgiven him and was calling him to come up and eat.

"Yes?" he said after a moment.

"What took you so long to answer?" she asked.

"I fainted from hunger, that's what."

"Hah-hah-hah," she said, imitating a laugh. "Some joke. *Nobody* fainted."

Yussie gave the counter another slap and got up. Then he went to the back of the store and shook his fist upstairs. "Listen, you," he said. "If I'm Mr. Nobody, then you must be Mrs. Nobody...."
Something came flying down at him. *Angel food cake!* he thought, forgetting to duck out of the way.

Yussie blinked around the room. What was he doing in a hospital? And why was his leg in a cast? He couldn't remember anything. Then he heard his wife's voice in the hall, and he remembered everything.

It *was* angel food cake. But the cake was still in the pan; the pan hit his leg; his head hit the wall; he fell over and he was knocked unconscious.

"I brought you some cake," Rosie said, coming through the door.

She put a paper napkin with the cake on Yussie's table and sat down in the chair near the window. Then she took her handkerchief out of her pocketbook and began to fan herself with it. She sat staring at Yussie's cast.

"Thank God things like that don't happen to me every day," she said.

Yussie looked at her. "To you? It's my leg!"

"And who had to pick you up? And who went for the doctor?" She gave a deep sigh. "Some luck I have," she said and fanned herself some more.

Her leg! Yussie thought. *Her luck!* The only thing that was hers was the *pan*. He would have liked to tell her off. But there were sick people around. She would only start yelling and disturb them. He pinched off a piece of cake and began to nibble at it, when the door opened and Zalman came in.

"My dear friend," Zalman said, giving Yussie a big hug.

How glad Yussie was to see Zalman! He slid his good foot out of the way, so Zalman could sit on the bed. Zalman and Red Rosie pretended not to see each other. She looked out the window, fanning herself. And he sat with his back to her, talking to Yussie and telling him jokes. After a while, Zalman got up. Keeping his back to Red Rosie, he said good-bye to Yussie and left.

A moment later, the doctor came in and stuck a thermometer in Yussie's mouth. "How's my patient?" he asked and began to examine Yussie. Yussie smiled. How could he answer? The doctor looked up at Red Rosie and said, "You'll be able to take him home on Friday. Take good care of him, now."

Red Rosie pulled her face over to the side and looked away. The doctor removed the thermometer, gave Yussie a slap on the back, and left.

Almost in the same moment, in came Faigle, Yussie's niece; Pat, the policeman; Heshy, the butcher; and Itsik, the barber. They stood around talking and laughing together in the crowded room until the nurse came in and asked them to leave.

The nurse left some pills and fixed Yussie's pillow. And no sooner was she gone when the landlord came in.

How it pleased Yussie to see the landlord. A busy man like that, coming to see him. The landlord spoke for a while about lazy plumbers and leaky pipes. Then he said good-bye to Yussie and wished him well. And he touched his hat to Red Rosie and went out the door.

"Since when is he a friend of yours?" Red Rosie asked.

"Who?" Yussie asked absently, thinking about all the nice people who had come to see him.

"Who! Who just left, the angel of death? Who do you think I'm talking about?"

"Oh, the landlord?" Yussie said. "Since always."

As the door opened, the Assemblyman came in. How honored Yussie felt. Such an important man! Even Red Rosie straightened up in the chair.

"I heard you were here," the Assemblyman said. "Feature that, my favorite constituent, laid up in the hospital. The street's not the same without you."

How good those words made Yussie feel. He looked over at his wife to see if she had heard.

The Assemblyman talked about the problems in the neighborhood and about the coming election. "Be sure to come and vote for me," he said to Red Rosie with a wink. Then he looked at his watch and said he had to go to City Hall. He said good-bye to Yussie. From the door, as he left, he saluted Red Rosie, as if she were a flag.

"What a nice man," Red Rosie said.

Yussie didn't answer. He wanted to think about all the people who had come to see him. And he turned to face the wall. Red Rosie knocked on his cast. He pretended not to hear, but she knocked again.

"You knocked?" he asked.

"Next time, *Mr. Nobody*," she said, "don't use

up all the hot water.''

Yussie couldn't believe he had heard right. That's why she knocked? To tell him that? He stared at her. Then he raised himself up on his elbows.

"Rosie," he said, "I'm telling you for the last time, never call me that again! You hear?"

Her face, which was usually pink, turned white. She looked at Yussie and nodded.

Yussie lay back down again. He looked up at the ceiling and began to smile. "You yourself saw today that I'm a somebody," he said. "Quite a few somebodies, in fact!" He used his fingers to count. "I'm a constituent, a friend, a patient, a tenant, a tax-

payer, I'm Faigle's uncle, I'm a neighbor, a customer, a locksmith—one of the best! And a husband," he said, looking at her. "I'm a husband,
too, Rosie," he repeated. Then he turned to the
wall and closed his eyes again.

For a moment the room was silent.

Then Rosie, speaking softly, in a voice he hadn't
heard her use for a long time, said, "Yussie?"

"Yes? he asked, turning to face her.

"Can I get you something from the canteen? A
glass of milk maybe? It's good with the cake."

From that day on she never called Yussie Mr.
Nobody again. Instead, it was "My husband,
Yussie" this and "My husband, the locksmith,"
that—wherever she went.

Feet In,

Feet Out

The Aristocrats of Sloof

People like to look at themselves. That's why there are mirrors. And cameras.

For friends, people choose others who look like themselves. That's why there are clubs. And associations. And cities full of people with short noses. And towns full of fools.

Sloof was such a town.

Pilger-the-peddler went from town to town selling spoons—coffee spoons, tea spoons, soup spoons—you name it. One day he arrived in Sloof. He had never been there before. To him, it was the next stop, another town, a place to sell spoons.

He brought his horse and wagon to a stop in front of the inn. What a surprise he had when he got down from his seat and looked around.

On one side of the street people were walking with their feet out. Like this:

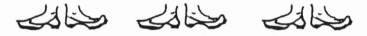

On the other side people were walking with their feet in. Like this:

Pilger didn't know what to make of it. He took his bundles and entered the inn. The thought of sleeping in a bed made him glad. The night before there had been no room at the inn and he had to sleep in his wagon.

The innkeeper, a heavy woman, was standing behind the counter.

Pilger went up to her. "Tell me," he said. "Why do the people here walk so funny?"

"What do you mean—*funny*?" she asked.

Pilger told her about the feet.

The woman came out from behind the counter. She stood with her right foot pointed to 3 o'clock and her left foot pointed to 9 o'clock.

"Those fools!" she said. "They stick their feet in, and think they're aristocrats!"

Pilger looked down at her feet. "I notice your feet stick out," he said.

The innkeeper gave a short bark of a laugh.

"This is how a true aristocrat walks," she said.

Pilger saw what was what and kept his mouth shut. He had come to Sloof to sell spoons, not to make enemies.

"You have a room for me?" he asked.

She pointed upstairs and gave him a key. Pilger picked up his bundles and went up the stairs. He remembered that it was the end of the month. Time for his wife to pay the rent. He had to send her some money at once.

Pilger leaned over the bannister. "Can you send me somebody to write a letter for me?" he called down.

"I'll get Velvel-the-orphan," the innkeeper answered.

Soon Pilger heard a knock on the door.

"Come in," he called.

Velvel entered with a small writing case. Pilger watched the boy walk across the floor and sit down at the table. Velvel's feet were straight!

"How come you walk straight?" Pilger asked.

Velvel smiled. "I guess I'm not an aristocrat," he said.

"What is it here, with the feet and the aristocrats?" Pilger said.

"There are two main families here," Velvel said. "One thinks aristocrats walk with their feet in, the other says they walk with their feet out."

"Two families?" Pilger asked.

"Large families," Velvel said. "Cousins marry cousins..."

"I see..." Pilger said. He looked at Velvel. "How can you stand it here?" he asked.

Velvel took a pad and pencil from his pocket. "I don't mind. I write poems," he said. "They don't come near me. If they pass me on the street, they dip their bodies the other way."

"Don't you get lonely?" Pilger asked.

"No," Velvel said. "The writing keeps me busy. And the poems keep me company."

Pilger stuck out his feet and slapped himself on the belly. *"Oi!"* he said.

Velvel laughed. The sound had taken him by surprise. He had never heard himself laugh before.

"Nu," Pilger said, looking at the ceiling. "Thank you, God, for leading me to Sloof. If the people here want to be aristocrats, I know just what they need. And thanks for sending me Velvel. With his help, I'll be able to pay the rent and maybe even buy my wife a new winter coat."

"How can I help?" Velvel asked.

"I'll tell you later," Pilger said. "First, let's write a letter to my wife."

Velvel took out a pen and some ink.

"Dear wife," Pilger began.

Velvel wrote down everything that Pilger said. Pilger told his wife where he was. He sent her money and told her to give half of it to the landlord. With the other half, he told her to buy a number of things, naming each one.

Velvel finished writing, and gave Pilger the letter to sign.

"You said something about my help before?" Velvel said.

Pilger took him by the arm. "I have an idea," he said. "How would you like to be my partner, my friend?"

Velvel shivered with delight. No one had ever called him friend before. His eyes shone as he sat listening to Pilger spell out the details of the plan.

Pilger the Aristocrat

In the morning, Pilger took a box of spoons and went to sell them to the pharmacist. The pharmacist bought two spoons. Pilger told him they were lump pressers. You'll soon see why.

Pilger and Velvel waited for the things Pilger had ordered to arrive. As they waited, Velvel taught Pilger the alphabet and how to sound out easy words.

In a few days, lots of cartons and boxes arrived. Pilger, Velvel and the wagon-driver dragged them all up to Pilger's room and stacked them up neatly against the wall.

"The play begins," Pilger said to Velvel, and ran out into the hall. He leaned over the bannister to speak to the innkeeper, who was standing and speaking with some of her feet-out cronies.

"I'm expecting A VERY IMPORTANT PERSON," he called down. "He's coming with his SERVANT."

The innkeeper nodded, and went on talking.

Pilger closed the door behind himself and opened a box. He took out a grey tunic, grey stockings, a grey hat, and a frilly yellow shirt.

"Here, put these on," he said, tossing them to Velvel.

Pilger opened another box and took out a long white fur cape, a pair of shiny black boots, and a yellow hat in the shape of a crown. He put them on.

The two partners looked at each other and laughed.

"Let's go," Pilger said, taking hold of a long walking stick.

"Wait!" Velvel cried. "The people here know me. They'll recognize me."

"No, they won't," Pilger said. "Fools don't look in a person's face. They look at what he wears."

"But the innkeeper knows us," Velvel said.

"Don't worry," Pilger said. "She'll think we're Pilger's guests, and that she didn't notice us come in."

Pilger pushed open the door and stepped out into the hall.

"Goodbye, Pilger!" Pilger shouted into the empty room. Then he bent over at the waist, like a broken toothpick. Velvel lifted up the back of Pilger's cape and followed him down the stairs.

The innkeeper and her feet-out cronies stared and bowed.

Outside, everyone stopped to look at Pilger and

Velvel. They presented quite a sight, Pilger bent in two and Velvel walking behind him and holding the hem of the cape. They walked to the town square, to the edge of the woods, then back to the town square again. Then Pilger went into the pharmacist's shop.

By plan, Velvel remained outside. He knew the Sloofians would soon appear with their questions. And as he waited, he studied the sky. It was blue as could be. A small, white cloud looked down at him. Velvel made a note to write a poem about it later.

A moment later, the Sloofians began to arrive, one by one. Each conversation Velvel had was a twin of the one before it.

"Who is the gentleman in the pharmacist's shop?" Velvel was asked.

"A great nobleman," he replied.

"Why does he walk that way?"

"He is an aristocrat. All aristocrats walk that way."

"What is he buying in there?"

"A lump presser."

"A lump presser? What is that?"

"If you were an aristocrat, you'd know what it was."

At last Pilger came out.

Velvel went behind Pilger to lift the hem of the cape. "You were right," he whispered. "They all wanted to know who you were and what you were buying."

"Good," Pilger said. "Now let's get back to the inn, and wait."

Pilger hobbled along. "*Oi!* My feet are killing me," he said. "My wife didn't have enough money for boots, so she sent me hers. They're way too small..."

"Look," Velvel said.

Pilger and Velvel could hardly keep from laughing. Already half the town was walking bent over at the waist. A man bent like a broken toothpick came rushing up to Velvel.

"What did the aristocrat buy in the pharmacist's shop?" he asked in Velvel's ear.

"A lump presser," Velvel whispered back.

"What is that?" the fellow asked.

"It's for aristocrats," Velvel said. "Walking the way they do, they sometimes bang their heads and get lumps. They press down the lump with a lump presser."

"Hmmmm, lump presser," the fellow said, rushing off.

"Let's hurry," Pilger said. "My back is killing me too."

Next to the inn was a dark alley. Pilger and Velvel ducked inside, took off their outer clothes and rolled them into a bundle. Pilger took off his wife's boots and straightened up.

"My feet and my back are sending me kisses," he whispered to Velvel as they entered the inn.

Spoons for Sale

Five minutes after Pilger and Velvel entered the room there was a knock on the door. Pilger ran to open it.

The pharmacist, a feet-in aristocrat, entered. He was out of breath from running.

Pilger shoved a chair under him. "What's up?" he asked, as if he didn't know.

"Rememer the lump presser you sold me the other day?" the pharmacist said.

"What about it?" Pilger asked, putting a little anger into his voice.

"I need more," the pharmacist said. "Lots more." He fanned himself with his hand.

Pilger winked at Velvel.

The pharmacist rose. "I can't believe it," he said. "Until I met you, I never heard of a lump presser. Now, suddenly, everyone wants one."

"Aha!" Pilger said. "Didn't I tell you it was a popular item?"

The pharmacist shook his head. "It's a regular epidemic," he said. "Every forehead has a lump. Everyone wants a lump presser."

Pilger glanced at the cartons against the wall. "How many do you want?" he said, trying to keep from sounding excited.

The pharmacist bought every carton. Not a spoon was left.

Pilger sat staring at the table. Velvel sat opposite him. The table was covered with money.

"Isn't that nice?" Pilger said. "Everybody's better off. I sold all my spoons. The pharmacist did a good business. And the people of Sloof have something new to think about."

Velvel smiled. "There's a new group of aristocrats here now," he said.

Pilger made two piles of the money and slid one pile over to Velvel.

"Here, partner, this is yours," he said.

Velvel slid it back. "I don't want it," he said.

Pilger stood up and looked at him. "But you earned it. It's yours," he said.

Velvel took two coins from the pile. "This is all I want," he said. "I'll buy some good writing paper."

Pilger scratched his head. "All right," he said, and started packing. "You'll come home with me. I'll open a store, and you'll be my partner."

Velvel got up. "Thanks, Pilger. But I'm staying here," he said.

"With all these fools?" Pilger said.

"I have a good life here. Nobody bothers me."

Velvel held up his pad and pencil. "This is all I want or need," he said.

Pilger stared at Velvel. Then he took him in his arms and gave him a hug.

"I never knew what a poet was," Pilger said. "It's a wonderful thing."

"I never knew what it was to laugh," Velvel said. "It's a wonderful thing." He tore a sheet from his pad and gave it to Pilger. "Can you read that?" he said.

Pilger squinted at the paper. He studied the words, then read aloud, slowly.

> *A slice needs a loaf,*
> *A moo needs a calf,*
> *A heart needs Pilger*
> *To teach it to laugh.*

Pilger brushed away a tear. He had never been able to read before.

"My house will always be open to you, if you change your mind," he said.

Then he tied the ropes around his valise. And he and Velvel went downstairs.

The innkeeper was bent over at the waist. She held a lump presser. Pilger looked at it.

"I know something about lump pressers," he said. "The one you have there is a dandy."

The innkeeper smiled. "I like only the best," she said. She looked at Velvel and shook her head.

"Look at this boy," she said. "He can read and write. But what good does it do him? He doesn't understand the first thing about aristocrats."

Pilger looked at Velvel. "Shame on you," he said.

Velvel smiled.

Pilger paid his bill. His horse and cart were outside. He put his bundles in back, and got up on the seat.

"Goodbye, and good luck, Velvel," he said.

"Goodbye, and thanks, Pilger," Velvel said.

Pilger clucked the horse onward.

"Goodbye, Feet-In and Feet-Out," Pilger called as the horse rode away. "My wife thanks you for the new winter coat."

He waved to Velvel, and rode on.

Ittki Pittki

Once in the great capital of Plil, there lived a rich merchant by the name of Ittki Pittki. For miles around there was no finer shop than his. His spices were the very best. His fabrics shone with perfection. The silks gladdened every eye. And if satins could stand up by themselves, his would surely have been able to waltz!

The merchant himself was small and round. He had two personalities. In the shop with his rich customers, he was forever smiling and making little jokes. And his cheeks were always rosy.

In back, where he lived with his wife and four sons, he barked, he didn't speak. And his face was the color of rain. If he smiled, it was only on Thursdays when his wife baked *ruggelach,* little pastries that he loved.

Now, on the hill in the center of the town lived

the Prince. Ittki Pittki's greatest honor was to serve the Prince. Just let him order the smallest thing. Let it be an inch and a half of silk to cover a button. Let it be a pinch of snuff. Would Ittki Pittki allow one of his sons to take it to the palace? Certainly not. Would he allow the Prince's own messenger to return with it? Never! In almost the same moment that the messenger arrived, Ittki Pittki would hurry out the door with the order.

Just as a swift-running river doesn't have to ask itself which way to flow, neither did Ittki Pittki. Never wondering about right or left, up the hill he sped until he came to the palace door. There, rejoicing in his good fortune, he would bow before the Prince and hand over the silk, or the pinch of snuff. In another moment he was running back to his shop to bark orders at his wife and sons.

One rainy morning, the shop was full of people. Ittki Pittki was clucking over a rich customer, showing her some green lace. His sons were busy at the spice counter. And his wife was measuring out twenty-two yards of brocade for the captain of a ship.

When the bell over the door tinkled, Ittki Pittki looked up to see who had come in. It was a messenger from the Prince! As if he were alone in the shop, as if the floor stood empty, he raced across the room to ask what the Prince wanted and flew out the door with a thimble.

Up the hill he sped in the rain, ignoring the mud and the puddles, holding the thimble under his tunic to keep it dry. In no time at all, he was at the palace door. When the Prince saw how wet the merchant was, yet how he had protected the thimble, he invited him to sit by the fire and have a glass of tea.

A glass of tea with the Prince! Ittki Pittki pinched himself to make sure he wasn't dreaming. Always before, he had *stood* in the Prince's presence. And then only for a moment. Now he was about to sit and—as if that weren't honor enough—have a glass of tea with him!

The Prince motioned to a chair. Although Ittki Pittki was wet through and through and his tunic stuck to his body, he tried to sit with dignity and grace. The Prince, facing him, spoke of one thing or another. Ittki Pittki listened attentively, allowing himself now and then—when the Prince looked away—to pull the wettest parts of his tunic away from his skin. Soon, a servant came with the tea. When Ittki Pittki raised the glass to his lips he nearly fainted. Floating in the cup was a tiny baby snake! Ittki Pittki didn't know what to do. If he mentioned the snake, the Prince would be embarrassed. If he refused to drink the tea, the Prince

would be offended. Ittki Pittki closed his eyes and drank down the tea.

Almost instantly he was seized by cramps. He tried to sit with dignity and grace, but the pains grew worse. When the servant came and led him to the door, it wasn't a moment too soon. He was doubled over with pain.

How he was able to get home is anyone's guess. Now he walked, now he stumbled, now he fell, now he crept. But at last he was home.

Shocked to see Ittki Pittki in such a pathetic state, his wife and sons got him into his night-clothes and put him to bed. They put a cold compress on his head and a hot-water bottle at his feet. And they sent for the doctor.

The doctor did not even bother to take off his hat. He took one look at Ittki Pittki and shook his head. There was nothing to be done, he told the family. Before long, Ittki Pittki would be dead.

The words chilled Ittki Pittki. Dead? Never see the sun rise again? Never hear the birds sing again? No more *ruggelach*? Ittki Pittki turned his head to the wall and let the tears roll down his cheek.

Without delay his wife and four sons talked to the funeral director, ordered a coffin, and put a *Closed* sign in the shop window. When they were through, they got into their mourning clothes and sat down in Ittki Pittki's room to wait. Night passed and morning came.

Ittki Pittki couldn't believe it when he heard himself hiccup. He thought surely he was dead. Had he only been dreaming then? He opened his eyes and saw the surprised faces of his wife and four sons looking back at him, and knew it wasn't a dream.

For another day and another night Ittki Pittki

continued not to die.

The following day, his wife and four sons left his bedside and opened the store; when Ittki Pittki got around to doing his part, they were ready to do theirs. Still in their mourning clothes, they got the store ready for business. Soon the bell over the door tinkled and a customer came in. Ittki Pittki, in the back, heard the sound. He was sure he would be

dead at any moment and that mourners were beginning to arrive. He listened to the voice, wondering who the mourner was.

It was the palace messenger! In a trice, he was out of bed and in the shop. Before anyone could even express surprise, he had snipped off the three-eighths of a yard of linen that the Prince had ordered and was flying up the hill with it. Just as a swift-flowing river doesn't have to ask the way, neither did Ittki Pittki. And soon he was knocking at the palace door..

When the Prince asked why he was wearing a nightshirt, Ittki Pittki was mortified. A nightshirt! And in the presence of the Prince! He apologized. Then he remembered *why* he was wearing a nightshirt, and he began to cry. He told the Prince the whole story, starting with the tiny baby snake and ending with the doctor and the funeral arrangements.

The Prince led Ittki Pittki into the large room and sat him down near the fire, where he had been sitting the last time. The Prince told him to calm himself, and gave him a glass of water to drink. Ittki Pittki raised the glass to his lips—and what do you think? Again he saw a tiny baby snake floating around inside!

This time, he showed the snake to the Prince. The Prince looked at it, and began to laugh. Then he pointed to the archer's bow that hung from the ceiling. Ittki Pittki looked up. The tiny baby snake was just a reflection of that bow!

Ittki Pittki was embarrassed. But he was also relieved. He was not going to die after all. He would see the sun rise again. And hear the birds sing again. And—his mouth began to water at the thought—eat *ruggelach* again come Thursday. With no thought whatever for dignity or grace, Ittki Pittki gathered up the hem of his nightshirt and ran home to cancel the funeral.

Ittki Pittki was so happy to be alive that from that time on he was a new man. Even at home he was forever smiling and telling little jokes. And even at home his cheeks were rosy.

The change in Ittki Pittki so pleased his wife that she began to make *ruggelach* on Mondays as well. But then, she liked them too. And so did the children.

Hardlucky

Once there was an unlucky fellow. So he thought of himself. And so he was.

If he was near a door, he caught his finger in it. If near a wall, he banged his head. If there was something on the ground, he stepped in it.

Hardlucky, they called him.

One day Hardlucky left his wagon standing on the hill and went to deliver wood. Now, why leave a wagon on a hill? Of course, when he got back, the wagon wasn't there. It had rolled down the hill— and hit a cow. Hardlucky was fined by the court, his boss took away the wagon, and Hardlucky was out of a job.

So it went with him. Poor Hardlucky.

Hardlucky went home, made a fire, and warmed himself by the fire. He sat for a while feeling sorry for himself. Then he heated up some soup and ate it, took off his shoes and fell asleep.

As he slept, a gust of wind blew down the chimney, whipping up the flames. First his shoes caught fire. Then the chair. Before long, Hardlucky was standing in the middle of the road scratching his head and gazing in disbelief at the ashes that had been his hut.

"Woe is me," he cried, seating himself on a stone and burying his face in his hands.

A blind beggar walked by and stabbed Hardlucky's foot with his stick. Hardlucky jumped up and grabbed the hurting foot. As he hopped around, he stepped on the tail of a passing dog, and the dog bit him in the other leg.

There and then Hardlucky decided to leave. He had bad luck here. Perhaps he would have better luck in another place. So thinking, he gathered a few stones with which to start building a house in the new place, wrapped them in a bundle, and set out for the river. With luck, he would find a boat to take him away.

He took not the regular road but the goats' road, because it was a shortcut. It was that, but it was also very steep. He slipped and slid, slipped and slid. When he saw a boat preparing to leave, he started to run, and fell. He couldn't get up again. And he rolled all the way downhill, his bundle bumping along after him. He landed at the pier in a heap.

"Mate!" the captain cried, looking over the side. "Some fool left two bundles on the pier. Go get them!"

The mate hurried down and soon returned with two bundles, which he placed before the captain.

The captain stood dumbfounded as one of the bundles uncurled itself and straightened up to become Hardlucky. Looking Hardlucky in the eye, he demanded to know why he had disguised himself as a bundle. Hardlucky said he hadn't disguised himself. And he explained how he had rolled downhill.

"Liar!" the captain shouted.

He stared at the second bundle.

"And I suppose you're going to tell me that this is not your traveling companion, but another bundle," he said, and gave the bundle a kick.

The captain broke his toe on the stones in the bundle and ordered Hardlucky arrested.

"Woe is me!" Hardlucky cried as they dragged him off.

Day after day, Hardlucky sat in the ship's prison. One morning, as the ship docked, two mates seized Hardlucky under the arms and flung him over the side.

"Good riddance!" the captain shouted as the ship sailed off.

Hardlucky found himself in a strange land. He looked around, wondering where he could be. The place was odd, and odd were its people. A group of them stood about, watching him. The smallest of the lot came toward him. A *street urchin,* Hardlucky thought.

"*Dja hav nyk oinz,*" the little fellow said, which in the language of the place meant, *Welcome.*

Hardlucky thought he had asked for coins. He turned his pockets inside out, to show he had none. "I'm sorry," he said.

Instantly, he was seized and thrown into jail.

Ahm sah ri in the language of the place meant, I spit on your land. To make matters even worse, the little fellow was no street urchin at all, but the mayor.

Hardlucky sat in jail, saying nothing and speaking to no one. In the morning he was taken by some guards to the border and shoved over to the other side.

By now, it mattered little to Hardlucky where he was. And it mattered even less where he went. But he couldn't just stand there. He had to move in some direction. So he turned his feet to the right and began to walk. And he walked and walked. When he could walk no more, he sat down near a clump of bushes and put his head in his hands. "Oh, woe is me," he wailed. "Woe! Woe! Woe!"

Now, it happened that on the other side of the bushes an old man was passing on his mule. The old man had been trying for some minutes to bring his mule to a halt. But the mule would not be stopped. Where the old man's kicks and slaps had failed, Hardlucky's voice had succeeded. For at his cry of *Woe!* the mule came to a sudden halt. The old man dismounted and went to look for the source of the voice. He saw Hardlucky on the other side of the bushes and went around to speak to him.

"Thank you for bringing my mule to a halt," he said. "Now I can rest for a moment." He looked at Hardlucky. "Tell me, young man," he added, "Why you are so unhappy?"

It had been such a long time since anyone had spoken kindly to Hardlucky that when he opened his mouth to speak he began to cry. And through his tears he told the old man about all his bad luck.

The old man smiled at Hardlucky. "I have good news for you," he said. "You are not unlucky at all."

Hardlucky looked up. "Not unlucky?"

The old man shook his head. "No," he said.

Hardlucky blinked.

The old man sat down next to Hardlucky.

Taking Hardlucky by the shoulder he said: "If you had stopped to think, none of those things could have happened to you. If you hadn't put your shoes near the flame, they could not have caught fire. And if you hadn't fallen asleep in the road, the blind man could not have stabbed you. If you had taken the regular road to the river, you would have arrived looking like a person and not like a bundle. As for the stones—why take stones from one place to another? There are plenty of stones everywhere.''

The old man nodded in the direction of the border. ''What happened over there could have been avoided, too,'' he said. ''If you had paid attention, you would have seen that the urchin was an old man. And you would have noticed that he was speaking a different language.''

Hardlucky smiled. ''Then I'm not unlucky?''

The old man smiled back. He shook his head. ''Just pay attention,'' he said as he rose to his feet. ''Stop to think. You will see how your luck will change.'' He then mounted his mule. ''I must be on my way,'' he said, and rode off.

Hardlucky was overjoyed. Then he wasn't unlucky, after all. If he paid attention, and he stopped to think, his luck would change. So thinking, he decided to return home.

Once more Hardlucky set out for the river. The old man's words danced in his mind. They made him feel so good, he began to run and jump and skip. Suddenly he tripped and fell. Hardlucky got up. As he looked around, he saw a sign reading, *Do Not Run, Jump, or Skip.* "You see?" he said, scolding himself. "If you had been paying attention, you would have noticed the warning."

Hardlucky promised himself not to forget the old man's words again. This time he walked carefully, looking this way and that. If he was drowsy, he pinched himself to keep awake. If he was near a door, he watched his fingers. If near a wall, he watched his head. If he saw something on the ground, he stepped around it. So doing, he arrived safely at the port.

He found a ship which was bound for his home and he asked for work. "What can you do?" asked the captain. Hardlucky was about to answer "Nothing." But he remembered the old man's words. And he stopped to think. If he said "Nothing," that's what he would get. So he said, "Whatever needs doing, if someone will show me how."

Hardlucky was taken aboard and put to work in the galley. He was taught first how to candle eggs. Then he was taught how to crack them on the side of a dish. He paid attention and learned well. Soon he could candle eggs along with the best. And crack them without looking.

They taught Hardlucky how to make a plain omelette. He memorized the steps: *Crack, beat, add salt, mix, drop into pan, watch, turn, watch, remove from flame.* He recited the steps in his sleep, too. When it came time to make his first omelette, he forgot the salt. But the next time he remembered. And soon he was making jelly omelettes and cheese omelettes and omelettes with fine herbs and all kinds of omelettes. Everyone on board agreed that Hardlucky had learned how to make the best omelettes that any of them had ever tasted.

The ship arrived in Hardlucky's home town. As a parting gift, the captain gave Hardlucky a hen. The crew gave him a frying pan. Thinking had become second nature to Hardlucky. And it didn't take him long to figure out what to do next.

He found some rocks along the pier and built a place to cook. He took an old wooden crate, turned it upside down, and called it a table. He made a sign reading OMELETTES. And before the day was out, Hardlucky had opened a restaurant.

News of the Hardlucky Omelette spread all over. The restaurant grew and grew. Soon the Hardlucky Omelette was famous throughout the town.

People still called him Hardlucky. No one could remember why anymore. Not even Hardlucky himself.